OTHER TITLES AVAILABLE FROM DANIEL WILLCOCKS:

The Rot Series

They Rot

They Remain

Keep My Bones

Short Stories

Flesh that Binds

The Other Stories Collections

Volumes 1-3:
Alien Invasion / Social Media / Zombies

Volumes 4-6:
Metamorphosis / Animal Attack / Coming of Age

Volumes 7-9:
Time Travel / Video Games / Contagion

Volumes 10-12:
Superheroes / Space / Under the Bed

Keep up-to-date at
www.danielwillcocks.com

Sins of Smoke

Daniel Willcocks

Copyright © 2017 by Daniel Willcocks

First published in Great Britain in 2015

with Hawk and Cleaver
www.hawkandcleaver.com

All rights reserved.

No part of this publication may be produced, stored in a retrieval system, or transmitted, in any form or by any means without the prior written permission of the publisher, not be otherwise circulated in any form of binding or cover or print other than that in which it is published and without a similar condition being imposed on the subsequent purchaser.

All characters in this publication are fictitious and any resemblance to real persons, living or dead, is purely coincidental.

ISBN-13: 978-1518611063

ISBN-10: 1518611060

www.createspace.com

For all who have supported me

— Sins of Smoke —

'Dear Father, forgive me for I have sinned.'

I hear the words leave my cracked lips; shaky, uncertain. Almost as though even the air leaving my lungs couldn't abandon me fast enough. I was alone, and I knew it better than anybody. Alone in this heap of shit chapel with no other option than to turn hypocrite and plead to a deity that I had spent my whole life mocking. For that's what people do when they've got nowhere to run, right? I'd seen it a thousand times in the movies. The bad guy runs to his nearest God centre – funny how they always manage to find one. I spent hours driving across this goddamn wasteland – he repents for his sins, then atones only to find karma ready to swing back around and smash his backdoors in (not in the faggot way). Then, boom! A cataclysmic circle of life. If you do bad shit, you'll get your punishment right? That's how it's supposed to be. But what happens when the boundaries blur? If I read between all the lines then I'm innocent in all this. So why the hell is it that I'm sat here now?

'I'm listening my child.' The words float through

the… trellis? (Hell I don't know what the correct term is… It's got to be some kind of trellis, right? That same stuff the gardeners use to encourage those creeper vines to find a tidier place to creep) and caressed my face. He has that calm, confident voice, flecked with the obvious tones of age that seems the custom of a preacher figure. I can see his outline. A bald head staring towards the ground. I can almost imagine that outta sight sits a newspaper, maybe his copy of the GOD LOVES ME TIMES, checking for his latest submission to the *St. Agony Aunt* column. 'Tell us your troubles, dear reader. We'll get you your answers from God.'

'I suppose, in a sense, my confession should start with the fact that this is my first confession. I've never had much cause to seek counsel before. Little happens in my shitty excuse for a town that would ever cause me to need the services of the Almighty. Folks in my end are as backwards as they can get. Even driving here seemed to skip me forwards thirty years, and now that I'm here it all kinda feels like a dream. All one big goddamn dream.'

'Language.'

'Language? Oh, shit. I mean, right! Blasphemy and all that… Sorry, Father.' I hunch over, embarrassed, and twiddle my crimson-specked Stetson between my fingers, examining the accumulated rips and stains from only hours before. Preacher pipes up.

'You are forgiven. Please, continue when you're ready.'

Feels strange to be given permission to speak, especially from a stranger. I've never been one to wait my turn and say my piece, that's just how I was made, ever since I was knee-high and clinging to Ma's skirt. Every time Ma would try to talk me down or tell me off I'd jump two steps ahead and push my own agenda. Pa used to laugh but it would drive Ma nuts. He always used to say to me 'Cooper. That mouth of yours'll get you out of more scrapes in life than any kinda fisticuffs. Sharpen that tongue and keep your hands clean. You'll go far.' Then he'd down his bourbon and leave for work.

The first rays of the morning sun pick their way through the stains on the window shining a full palette of colour in my cubicle. I see the same patterns trailing across the old preacher's face making him look like one of them Picasso paintings they hang in the truck stops off the main road to make the place seem all sophisticated.

'I'll be honest, I don't know how to begin this one. I mean, I know the procedure, but I just ain't sure how to order my words to make this make sense to you.'

'Why don't you just start from the top? After all, it makes the most sense to begin at the beginning' – sarcastic bastard. I like him.

I rub my fingers together feeling the roughness of the callouses, watching the faint dawn light shimmer off the scar that lines my palm, and try to figure my words.

I could try and tell the truth in the order that it happened, but who in their right mind would believe me? People in my backwater town don't pay no heed to supernatural shit and lynch any of those that do. Davy Thrisket learned that the hard way. I was only a kid at the time, but story went that Mr Thrisket was hooting and hollering about some demon that jumped into his kid one rainy day, and the mayor – at the time – caught him trying to smack the devil out the poor bastard. Suffice to say, old Davy was dragged out for the rope to protect the townspeople, and his kid, from harm's way. Medieval justice, eh?

If I take out all the facts then I'm labelled a murderer. Black and white. I sure as shit would call someone the same. But, fuck it, I ain't. I ain't no goddamn murderer. Anyone that saw the whole thing start to finish would agree, but ain't nobody saw it all but me. Shit. Preacher next door is sworn to secrecy, right? That's why all the walls and pretence?

'Anything I say stays between you and me, right?'

'Just about, my child—'

I cut him off real quick. 'No offense, Father. But I ain't really one for formalities. The name's Cooper, though everyone calls me Coop. Which'll make you Father…?'

'Father Harrison. And of course, Cooper. Anything you say stays between us and the Lord above.'

The Lord above. If I was a firm believer then maybe I'd feel some pressure at that. Nothing like airing all your dirty laundry in a verbal three-way, eh? Though I have to admit that despite my atheism I can feel something… ominous. Something under the glow of the dust specks floating in from the thin rays outside. After all, who am I to question what's real and what ain't? Not after last night. That shit turned my whole belief system upside-down. So, why not? Maybe I can open my mind enough to believe there may be something bigger above us, watching (doing a shit job in my eyes, but watching nonetheless). Maybe He can hear me right now. Maybe it's God right now turning up the heat, making me sweat like a roasted pig bathed in Jack Daniels. Or it could just be my conscience. The walls feel cool to the touch, though I feel like the Devil himself is giving me a backrub. That's crazy talk though, I'm sure God would have some rules in place to stop the Devil entering his holy house.

'Cooper?'

Right. He's waiting on my story. I suppose, in a way, I am too. Though I can't decide which angle to take. If anything I guess now would be the time to let Jesus take the wheel. I'll use my God-given gift and just talk. Whatever comes out my mouth is what I'll roll with, and I'll deal with the consequences later.

I ask Father Harrison if I may begin again. The light bouncing off his bald cap lets me know that that's okay.

'Forgive me, Father, for I have sinned. Last night I killed someone.'

'Oh?'

'Yeah. I killed a demon.'

*

Poor mama was sick. Though that's nothing unusual, she was always sick these days. Arthritis got to her a couple years back and that bastard had been clawing away ever since. But last night it seemed as though the air was fighting to leave her faster than she could hold it in.

She was sat in Pa's old rocking chair, for the

comfort of it. Before Ma started aching and hollering no one was allowed to sit in Pa's chair, and he made certain everyone knew. A couple of times as kids me and Kenny made a game of trying to steal a seat before he got home from work (until a couple of times we got caught and made it seen to we couldn't sit on his chair for a week – or any other chair for that matter).

I watched Ma, sat on the soft leather cushions, hunched over with her knitting needle like some kind of buzzard trimming its claws. She was silhouetted against the back window as the last dregs of the sun shone against the side of her face. I thought it strange, then, how the light made the one side seem so much younger. Almost as though time had slipped backwards and restored some of her youth. Yet, the shadows on the darkened half sent a chill down my spine, showing her frailty and the effects that age had sprung upon her. She was old now, and somehow came down with some kind of cold or ailment almost every other day. I wasn't ready for Ma to die.

Kenny came running down the stairs like someone had taped fireworks to his shoes and landed with a *thump* at the bottom. Shook me and Ma up real good as we ain't seen Kenny for a few days now. The layabout spent most of his time moping in his room since losing his missus to the doctor's son, Billy Richton. Not that I blame her at all. In my humble opinion you'd have to be scraping the bottom of the barrel to settle for my brother.

'You're never gonna believe it, Ma!' he cried, breathless from his dash. His shaggy hair clung to his sweaty forehead giving the impression he'd been out for a run. I had to laugh at the state of him. No stamina at all. Of course, he noticed. 'You best stop your mouth from flapping, 'fore I stop it for you.'

Kenny got madder when that made me laugh more. 'How the hell you gonna stop me flapping when you can't even hold your own lady down? You ain't got enough fight in you to get at me, brother. So why don't you take a breath and tell us what's got you so riled up. I ain't seen you this pumped since Dennis laced your toothpaste with coke.'

Dennis was the town prankster, and my best friend. He had the Pied Piper's charm with the ladies and the stealth of an underground rat to sneak up and play his jokes. Granted, the son-of-a-bitch sometimes went a bit too far with his shenanigans, but he somehow always found a way to make folks see the funny side. That was what was so dangerous about Dennis.

'When you gonna let that go, Coop? It was one time, okay? People have forgotten.'

'Just because people ain't say nothing, doesn't mean they don't remember. People don't forget in this town.' I loved to tease Kenny. It was like leading a pig down a shit-slide, and I had years of experience on my side to know how to push his buttons. Or maybe it was just his nature. He'd always had a short temper.

Ma paused her *click-clacking* and snapped at us. 'Boys! That's enough,' she squawked. 'I know I ain't got much puff in my billows but I'll use everything I got to come over there and whoop you both. I don't need this kind of racket breaking such a sunset. Now, what is it you want, Kenny?'

'Right! Turns out Sarah and Billy been at each other's throats ever since she found him peeping through Darleen's bushes, and she wants to meet me at the Coyote to talk things over.' I couldn't believe his excitement. The way he was talking like she could do no wrong, forgetting the last time she broke his heart and trampled it into the dust. That would never be me. Ever since Pa left without leaving so much as a note for Ma I promised myself I'd never hand my heart to nobody. What's mine is mine. You'd think Kenny was some kind of cat the way he handed his out like he had some to spare.

Ma croaked something positive about Kenny being a lucky bastard for having a second chance with a lover and I saw the effect those words had on him. Next to Ma it was Kenny who took Pa's leaving the hardest. As the eldest son they'd always been close and it was a tough role to place the master of the house on him when he was so young. And I swear if I hadn't been in the room right there and then those watery eyes of Kenny's would have shed. Not that he ever wanted to show his affectionate side around me.

'If you're heading out, mind if I come along? The gang should be up to their mischief soon and you know how I hate being the last to arrive. I hear Dennis has some surprise lined up for you too,' I shot him a wink that met an icy return. He really doesn't get my humour.

Then Ma coughed. I ain't ever heard a cough like it in my life. It racked her body and curled her up in a ball, looking like an armadillo but sounding like a rattlesnake was trying to escape her gut. I really didn't like to leave after hearing that.

But Ma insisted. I don't care what anybody says, no matter how old you get, you never wanna say no to your mama. After years of losing arguments and being told that mama is always right, it kinda sticks.

So we left. Me and Kenny. We didn't feel all that great leaving Ma alone but we both knew she'd be happier in peace, left to her knitting. Following the old dirt path we used to tread as kids we made our way to the Coyote. In some ways it felt like we were those kids again, and we laughed and teased and talked about Kenny's chances in romance and the possibilities that night could hold.

*

I lose my tongue for a moment and look at the floor. For the first time since I arrived I allow my senses a moment to breathe. Harrison notices the silence yet allows me a few moments of reflection. Classy guy. I wish I'd have a chance to thank him when this is all over, but I don't see that as an option. The musky scent of stale beer seduces my nostrils, rising from the splashes that, even now, feel sticky to the touch on my trouser leg. There's something else in those dark patches that I don't care to remember. The weak man's fluid. But I'll move past that.

My cap hangs loosely in one hand as I wipe the gathering sweat from my brow with the other. The sun is rising in the sky now and I can feel the heat causing further discomfort besides the aches and bruises that dot my body. Seems like every part of this damned booth is made of some kind of wood. I guess they don't expect long-staying visitors in here. I remove my jacket and scrunch it up under my butt in an attempt to both cool down and find some kind of comfort. After all, I've only cracked the surface.

*

By the time we approached the Coyote the sun was already beginning to set. I could hear the howls of the gathering prairie dogs on the nearby hills, waiting to prey on those brave enough to step outside alone at night (like some poor asshole would ever do that again). As me and Kenny walked that last half mile we played with our shadows, making them dance and hit each other on the dusty trail below. It was like we were kids again, play fighting and laughing in a way in which we ain't in years, and won't ever do again.

Before we knew it we were outside looking up at the swinging post of the Coyote – a white silhouette of the beast howling in front of a large, black moon – and the place was alive. Even from the outside we could see the shapes of a hundred thirsty locals, and hear the cries and clanging of glasses from every fucker inside. I tell you, there ain't nothing can compare to that place. It's like all your birthdays come at once every time you step through that door.

'Cooper!'

'Kenny!'

'Over here!'

There really weren't no point in them shouting.

You'd have to be blind not to notice the crowd gathered round the hive of activity in the centre of the bar. If it wasn't for the smiling faces of Shackles and Tommy jutting out above the sea of heads I'd wonder what was going on, but this was his favourite party trick. I'd seen it a thousand times before and, though I couldn't see his face, I knew the signs. The way they both held his legs and raised him upside-down in the air. He was famed for shining in the spotlight and couldn't ever miss the opportunity to clown around.

Kenny scoffed his disapproval and quickly lost himself in the crowd. Even though he says he's moved on I know he ain't ever forgiven Dennis. Not really. Dennis could be cruel at times but he always seemed to crack down harder on my brother for some reason. He says it's nothing, but he always seemed a little green at the fact me and Kenny were brothers by blood, and not just by voice.

Working my way through the crowd was tough. Those folks were packed around tighter than an elephant in a barrel, but I managed to peek through and confirm my theory.

Dennis.

Of course it was Dennis. The guys were stood on chairs and circled him like a tepee, supporting his legs as he attempted to drain as much of the supporting keg as he could through a tube – and the crowd were loving it. You could see the familiar sparkle in Dennis's eyes as the circle whooped and cheered, clapping their hands loudly to encourage the bastard to continue. I couldn't help but join in and smile. As he gulped and spluttered you could see the excess liquid that failed to enter his throat leak out his mouth and up towards his nose, frothing his face like a dog with rabies.

And that's when I saw.

It happened in seconds. As I stared into the reddening face and looked beyond the amber liquid waterfall I noticed his eyes, no longer focusing on the crowd ahead. The spluttering increased with every passing second as his body began to reject the drink it could no longer handle. All around the faces watched and clapped on expectantly, but Dennis could no longer see them as his eyelids stopped fighting back against the tide and he lost consciousness. The spluttering slowed.

I began to fight through the few that remained in front of me to reach the inner circle where my friends continued to hold his increasingly limp form aloft like a 180lb prize catch, blissfully unaware, caught up in the euphoria. But this wasn't part of the act. I had seen it enough times to know how it ended, and I ain't never seen him take it this far.

'Shacks! Tommy! Put the fucker down!' I screamed, much to the annoyance of the perimeter that surrounded us. But I was oblivious to them, with only one objective on my mind. I didn't give a pig's scrotum if I was ruining their fun, I just needed to make sure he was okay.

'Christ's sake, can't you see he's not breathing! Put him down, now! Jesus! Gently. Easy now. Dennis? Dennis?!' I hollered at his face, hoping to get some movement or recognition from those glazed eyes and found nothing in return. I scanned the crowd, hoping to find someone who would be able to help in the ways I couldn't. I'm no doctor by any scratch, and I ain't never done none of that resuscitation shit. Any pet I've ever got ended up dying on me by the end of the week by 'mysterious' circumstances. I knew that if it was down to me to pump his stomach, he had no hope.

From outta the sea of confused faces he came. Swifter than death on horseback the plump figure of Mr Sam Richton crouched down beside me, froth still littering his heavy walrus moustache. I tell you, I ain't never been so thankful to see him. Usually a visit with the old town doctor meant some serious shit. It was usually best to avoid a visit to Papa Medicine out there, where his stockroom of ointments and potions only really managed to stock enough for the elderly and the young. But yesterday, I could not have been happier to see his face, and I could not give one single shit how pissed up he may or may not have been.

He had a calm voice. You know, the kind of guy who could walk into a room and just settle folks down (though, that may be as folk just respected him too). But I knew I was in the safest of hands when he spoke. 'Hold him steady, Cooper, and don't be alarmed.' Peering over his half-moon spectacles he prodded and poked Dennis's stomach, looking for that sweet spot. Then, quick as a flash, brought his clenched fists down hard on his chest, pulsing a loud *thud* through the bar. As skin met skin and Dennis's chest caved inwards his lips puckered with an escape of air. Completing the fish image, his body writhed and squirmed as a giant plume of foam shot out into the air above him, hovering for the briefest of moments before falling back towards the ground and slapping Dennis in the face. His eyes snapped open and he sat up sharp, taking massive drags of air (between coughs) and looked around him wildly.

If I hadn't been there myself, I wouldn't have believed this next part to be true. But, being one to always think quick on his feet, the moment that Dennis realised where he was, the fucker stood up and bowed!

I wish I could've taken some kind of picture to capture that moment. With his nose inches from the floor with his drunken curtsy the crowd exploded into a mass of cheers. The former foundations of the Dennis wigwam continued their ignorance to his (near fatal) mistake, hugging and celebrating like it was all a new part of the act, designed to keep the routine fresh for audiences. Mr Richton rolled his disapproving eyes, yet patted the star of the show on the back before returning to his table where his wife sat dumbfounded. I mean, the whole tavern was on a high, and at that point I think people worried that the night might have peaked too early.

Stumbling to the nearest table, Dennis parted the sea of bodies before him. At this point, I could see the effects of his trick taking hold of him. It must've taken a hell of a lot of alcohol to make a man as blurry eyed as Dennis was. He sat before me, and I could see the telltale signs of a man who had drunk his fill, and gone beyond what his body could handle. Even after he sat down you could see the drink leaking out his mouth and onto his collar, leaving golden stains as it went.

'Hold right there, brother, I'll get you something to

wipe yourself clean.' His eyes made contact with mine, seemingly for the first time that night, harbouring just the smallest amount of recognition at my arrival.

'Co-*hick*-op' he hiccupped, splatting large chunks of saliva in my face. 'Goo ta see-*hick*-ya, bud. Whe d'you ge-*hick*-here?' He smiled that lazy smile that comes with drink, making him looking like a reflection of himself in one of the magic mirrors they sell at the joke shop. I wondered if that was how he saw me through his beer-tinted lenses.

'Made it just in time to see your grand finale you crazy bastard. Though, it certainly ain't as I remembered it. Gave me one hell of a fright there, Den. You can buy me a pint to settle my nerves,' I winked at him and headed to the bar, leaving him to gaze drunkenly at his feet while I grabbed some napkins from old Rusty the barkeep. Rusty is a good sport when it comes to shenanigans in his bar – probably the reason we keep going back – but he always seemed to have that special soft spot for us. Whether we reminded him of himself as a kid, I don't know. All I know is that in the Coyote, we could get away with murder, and Rusty would mop up the floor behind us.

I took the liberty of buying a couple of pints on Dennis's tab, gave a quick nod to Kenny who was sat with a sobbing Sarah on his shoulder (I thought it best not to cramp his style), and arrived back to find the guys mid-way through their play-by-play with a semi-conscious Dennis hanging over Pete's shoulder. Pete – being the sensible one among us – had taken good sense to supply Dennis with water to help relieve some of his dizziness. Although Den was still dribbling and drooling like a baby fresh off its mother's tit all over Pete's crisp work suit, he didn't seem to mind. It was the end of the work week, and Pete knew his missus would take care of any stain or scuff that may be accumulated from his weekend antics. Irene was good like that. The true mark of a good woman.

I entered the cacophonic circle and wiped my buddy's face. He still seemed to be in the room with us at this point – always a good sign – and although his hiccups still shook with every other syllable his eyes seemed clearer and more aware than before. Placing myself on a free stool I checked around the room for the first time since my arrival. The aftermath of Dennis's stunt was wearing off as punters returned to their tables, picking up their conversations and adding their own contributions to the surrounding din of the Coyote. Shit, I loved that place. It was like a second home to me. Even if you couldn't hear yourself think at least you knew you were never alone. As I looked around at the gang, each fighting to be heard over one another, I remember feeling that warm sense of satisfaction. Home. All six of us. A family.

It's hard to say how the group formed. An unlikely gathering of misfits drawn together, probably by the influence of your great God Almighty. All I remember is that one day it was just me and Dennis, and the next there was six. Me, Den, Tommy, Pete, Shacks and Suds. We were a good crew, living on that sweet spot between lovable and lawless, and somehow people just warmed to us, waving off our mischief like we were ten-year-olds smacking a hoop with a stick. I put most of this down to the fact we always stayed polite and, between the six of us, we knew half the town well enough for them to know we didn't mean no harm. I mean, why would we? That town ain't seen trouble in decades. Unless you believe the tales and legends the kids told. But you forget about those when you're grown. They're all just stories, right? Though, now that I'm sat across from you one springs quite strongly to mind. It tells of an old preacher man. The rumour ran that he'd started holding kids back in Sunday school and was touching them in a way that no man of the church ever should, before running out of town only for the authorities to find his body out in the wasteland weeks later, foam coating his lips and eyes rolled in the back of his head.

If you can believe such shit! A kid's cautionary tale that circulated the youth of the town. Ghost stories saved for a full moon and a sleeping bag at a friend's house. Although that tale started finding its way around the schools when I was a kid no one ever paid it much heed. It was hardly unusual in a town as isolated as that for people to come down with something and for whispers to turn the flu into some wild supernatural tale of death and fear.

But overall things were at peace. I ain't saying bad stuff *never* happened. There's always gonna be that one couple that take a fight too far, or some family grudge that finds its conclusion. Or sometimes accidents happen, Shackles can tell you as much. He's our muscle. That guy wound up in juvy more times than he can count on his fingers and toes, yet he was mostly innocent. Just got in with the wrong crowd and sometimes let his temper get the better of him. He'd never go so far as killing a guy, but I'll have to admit that he has some trouble understanding the limits of his own strength. (More than once I've come away with a sprained wrist from a high-five). But he seems to have settled with us and, touch wood, he ain't seen the other side of the iron bars since he was legal to drink.

'Man, that's gotta be about the best performance you ever done give, Den. You and Coop must've been planning that shit for months.' Tommy was easy to fool.

'Ah, c'mon-*hick*-Tommy. You're-*hick*-making me-*hick*-blush.'

'Did you see the looks on folks' faces? That was definitely one for the highlight reel! Though, you had me worried when you came busting in Coop. I ain't never pegged you much for an actor.' Shacks eyed me suspiciously at that point. I looked to Dennis for help.

'Think whatever the-*hick*-hell you like, *Finchley*'. Their eyes met as a flush of anger rose to Shacks' cheeks. Shackles hated his Christian name and Dennis knew it. Part of me was grateful for the distraction, but damn it I told Den enough times not to push his buttons. Before Shacks could say anything Dennis continued. 'But, at the end of the-*hick*-day, who's the one who-*hick*-managed to get-*hick*-bladdered for next-*hick*-to nothing? *Hick!* Even managed a-*hick*-free pint off-*hick*-Coopy boy.' He winked in my direction, I winked back, warm in the belly from the pint he paid for. I liked to have my fun too.

'I'm just saying, Den. One of these days

something's gonna go too far. All this pratting around at our ages, we ain't as young as we used to be. Especially you. You're like one of them old Fords. The more mileage you get, the more likely you are to break down!' The table exploded with laughter.

'Ah, go easy on him guys. At least wait until he's pissed out some of that keg and can see straight again, eh?' joked Pete. 'We can point and laugh when he zigzags to the john,' he added, nudging Dennis gently in the ribs.

'Who says I haven't-*hick*-already been?' Dennis smiled goofily, nodding towards his crotch where a small, dark wet patch stood out amongst his light, dust-coated trousers.

'You *haven't*?!'

'Oh my God, he has!'

'Ha! This is too much!'

Even I had to join as I recoiled from the table, clutching my aching sides. 'C'mon, Den. Gone a bit far this time, haven't we?!'

Above the din Dennis rose sharply. 'Of course I-*hick*-haven't! Ha! *Hick!* Old shaky-hands Pete-*hick*-missed my mouth didn't he. He's got the-*hick*-aim of a drunken school-*hick*-girl!' And with that said he headed for the men's room, leaving behind the red-faced Pete, coughing and spluttering his beer as the rest of the guys howled with laughter.

*

I swear to Him upstairs, judging by the events of things

at that moment, I believed that nothing could bring us down. Everyone was as high as can be, ain't nobody could say otherwise. A few drinks further down and our brains were getting as hazy as the naked bulbs on the ceiling, barely visible through the swarms of night bugs that hovered around the electric pulses, harmless to all, but annoying as shit whenever you stood. All around us people would walk by and nod their 'hellos', pat Dennis on the back and make some kind of remark that inflated his ego larger than a hot air balloon. You could see the satisfaction in his unfocused eyes as he paid no heed to Pete's advice and carried on with his drinking. It was almost like he was hunting for trouble, but where would trouble find us? We were solid as a group. Untouchable, defiant and cocky. Everyone had brought their A-game and were pitching jokes, quips and tales like they were going outta fashion.

All that is, except Suds.

Now, Suds wasn't usually the most verbal among us. In fact, he could be downright frustrating. I suppose it's not seen as all too much of a bad thing, but Suds was obsessed with his hygiene. Always had been. In fact, that's where he got his name from. Suds would always scrub those bubbles until his skin shone bright enough to light the room before he left for anywhere, so most of the time the fucker was late. Of course, he hated his nickname, but it stuck pretty quick. 'Never give people cause to give you a shitty nickname,' my father once warned me after me and Kenny were trying out a few. 'Nicknames are like VD. Once you have one, it'll follow you around forever.' Though, I like to think of myself as the exception. Years back (I'm talking toddler days) I earned the nickname 'Skid'. I won't give you any prizes for guessing what that may relate to, but let's just say that that shit stuck on the underpants of my life for years. The only way I managed to escape it was when I was hitting my pubescent years and met a young Dennis. That son-of-a-bitch saved my soul by making a blood promise with me that he'd take down any fucker bold enough to use that name through school. (At that point I didn't know what a blood promise was, but who was I to argue? He offered a saving grace and already had the crimson jam pouring out the slice in his palm before I'd had the chance to say no). In exchange, I just had to give him my loyalty. That's all. He was a lonely kid before he drank that big bottle of *I-don't-give-a-fuck-juice* that sometimes comes with the hormones and he turned into the cheeky fucker we know him as today.

But I digress.

In all the raucous it was easy to miss Suds.

*

At this point in the night the sun had already said it's farewells to the day and sunk behind the lonely hills. Outside the air was still and quiet. The temperature had dropped dramatically the minute the orange light had been replaced by the silver of the moon, meaning wildlife of the night could come outta hiding, sneaking through the darkness like shadows. Besides the fading echoes of the voices falling outta the Coyote, little dared disturb the night as it waited in anticipation.

'C'mon, Sudsy! If you love it so much, why don't you marry it? You've been teasing that pint since we sat down. Get it down your neck, get your ass off your chair and pay up. It's your round!' Tommy's call was met with loud agreement from the rest of the group.

'Yeah, Suds. What's eating ya? Nearly forgot you were here!'

'You look a bit peaky, bud. I mean, more than usual. D'ya scrub a bit too hard?!'

The jest met the expressionless wall. It was light-hearted taunting, we were famous for it, though Suds failed to look impressed. Wordlessly he drained his glass and walked towards old Rusty who greeted him in the same way that he greeted everyone. With that warm, toothless smile.

'What d'ya think's got his back up?' Pete posed the question, not really expecting a serious response.

Tommy was the one to reply. 'Must've missed bath time. He ain't exactly up to his usual standard, is he? Maybe Rebekkah has smacked him round again!'

Shacks laughed between mouthfuls of golden froth. 'He ain't never been the one to wear the trousers in that house!'

I'm not sure if it was the warmth of the beer spreading through my body or just a general wave of pity that hit me at that moment, but I found my eyes wandering over to the bar where the back of Suds' head hung low over the sticky, wooden counter. Flecks of grey spotted the rug of hair that always seemed immaculately groomed, like it was glued in place. Though Tommy was right. Last night, for the first time since I'd known him, it stood all skewwhiff like he hadn't touched it in days. I wondered then what kinda demons must be playing on his mind, and I felt sorry for him.

Ignoring the din of the group I decided to join Suds at the bar. Sometimes all you need when you got your mind buzzing with bees is someone to talk to and blow the bastards out, and since no one else seemed in any way inclined to play the supportive pal I figured I was the best shot he had.

Weaving through the trail of chairs with no tables to belong to I noticed how much quieter the bar had become. Rusty seemed not to mind in the slightest as he stood chatting to a familiar face (with a name that escaped me), polishing his glasses and taking a well-earned breather. I've never understood why he always insisted on running the place himself. Maybe it was a pride thing. He didn't want to relinquish control and admit that maybe his time was coming up. I'm not sure how that old grandfather clock kept ticking to be honest. Lucky he was as loved around here as everybody's grandpa cause I heard the way that people complained about the speed of his service (though never to his face), but despite their misgivings the punters would smile and say the right things before growling under their breath as they took the drinks to their table.

Taking a seat next to Suds I glanced along the bar noticing the absence of my brother and his fancy-bitch. (He hates it when I call her that, but, fuck it, he ain't here).

'They left about half hour ago Mr Cooper'. I

couldn't help but smile – *Mr*. He was always polite like that, bless his soul. 'Seemed to be in a real hurry too. Saw them whispering some words to each other then they darted out that door swifter than a couple of bunnies in heat.'

'My brother never could keep it in his pants. Spends so much time drooling over gals it's no wonder he gets himself in so much trouble. What about you, Rusty? You must've been quite the catch in your day.'

'This here is still my day Mr Cooper', he said, accompanying the remark with a hearty chuckle. 'You wanna see the amount of gals pining for old Rusty's bones. Where the water hole is tapping, the young ladies come lapping.' With another loud laugh his attention was caught by another customer waiting.

Suds sat quietly, staring into the tray of drinks he'd purchased, and we spent a few moments in silence. Funny how sometimes not saying anything can sound respect ten times louder than actions, eh?

'Boy... Richton's gonna be pissed when he gets wind of where my brother is poking it tonight. Kenny always has cared more about his little head than his big one.' I let out a small laugh, hoping to lighten the mood and put a smirk on his face. Suds gave me nothing.

'Course, he should be careful really. If Sarah left him once, there's nothing to say it couldn't happen again. You ain't heard any reason that those two should be fighting, have you?' It was a longshot, but you know how gossip spreads in a small town.

Still nothing. Suds continued to stare and blink at the amber-coloured glasses with the rapidly disappearing heads.

'Y'know, if you're not careful those'll get flat soon. The guys don't take kindly to flats,' I addressed him directly this time, hoping to break the shell. I was on a mission now. I didn't like the stony silence that met my words.

'Fuck 'em' came the slow reply. He sounded half cut, though I couldn't say that I'd seen him drink more than one full glass, and there was something in the dark glimmer in his eye that put me on edge.

That caught me off-guard. I had no idea how to follow that. Suds was never the wildest of us, in fact, he was always rather placid, and if he'd ever taken issue with the group he'd never shown it. But I was taken aback then by the menace scribbled on his unshaven face. All I could find in response was a short, 'huh?'

'You heard me, Coop. Fuck 'em. I'm sick of the lot of them, pissing around, acting like they ain't got a care in the world. It's a dangerous place out there for fools and jesters.' His eyes flickered briefly to where Dennis sat wobbling dangerously as the guys busied themselves playing a game of *stack-a-tower* out of the empty glasses Rusty had failed to procure. 'They don't see it now, but their time will come.'

'What's gotten into you, Suds? Is it Rebekkah? Is everything right at home?'

'Let's just say this...' He paused, taking a large mouthful of beer. Whether this was for dramatic effect or not, I don't know, but I found myself hanging on his every word. 'There's plenty of time tonight for that tower to topple and come crashing down.'

With that my attention was thrown back to the table as a wave of triumphant roars and crashes exploded with a stomping of feet. The tower that only moments before had shone with pride had come hurtling down, raining shattered glass across the floor like razor-sharp puddle drops. There was something almost too coincidental in the way Suds' words had matched the downpour, *almost as if he knew*. I shook away the thought.

Without so much as a sideways glance Suds slid his stool back and stood. He fumbled through his pockets for his wallet and threw a couple of tatty, green bills on the counter before walking towards a large wooden door at the far side of the bar. 'Coop? You coming', he beckoned in a voice that seemed to tell me that 'no' would not be an option.

For a moment I froze. Hell, I can't explain it. Whether it was fear or caution, I froze. Sue me. Something definitely wasn't right in Suds' character, and hindsight can be a bitch in illuminating your mistakes. But I did it. I followed Suds against my better judgement and walked through the heavy door marked PRIVATE. If Suds had something to get off his chest then let him. I'm all ears.

As I took those steps through the doorway I could hear the continued hoots and hollers from our table. Closing the door I caught the smiling face of Pete as he leant over the bar to grab Rusty's attention.

'Broom and mop in the usual place?' he grinned, displaying his best puppy-dog eyes.

'I'll put it all on your tab' Rusty smirked back, theatrically rolling his eyes.

It was all routine.

*

I find myself admiring the patience of the man in the booth next to mine. Can't be easy to listen to the ramblings of a nobody – that's how I see myself through his eyes. Thinking about it, I couldn't hold half the attention span that the old preacher showed if my own Pa came waltzing through the doors. I can see his sorry face now and I imagine him opening that door holding his arms out wide with that familiar smile that I used to love. I don't know how I'd be. I suppose I'd like to think I'd give him a chance to explain himself. Not that he'd have much chance to say anything before my fists did the talking. I can be impulsive like that.

The morning sun is well-established now, and a quick check outside shows the heat hitting the old dirt road, sending the terrain into a mystic wobble. Every nook and cranny inside the old church stands proud in the light for all to see as the dust-speckled rays of sun illuminate what was previously unseen. Despite the (did we settle with trellis? I'll say we did) trellis designed to give privacy between talker and listener, I am able to make out enough of his profile that I could pick the old man out in a lineup – should things ever come to that. There's something familiar in the lines that wrinkle across the old man's forehead, comforting even. That grandfather-sat-round-the-fire vibe.

The church bells begin to chime, breaking my chain of thought. A brass reminder that my time is running thin, and after reeling the old preacher in so far, I'd hate to disappoint. I waited for the ancient bell to stop ringing.

Silence followed the eight chime.

*

The room marked PRIVATE was poorly lit. Barely large enough to hold the table that centred it, the room was what the optimists would call cosy (and the pessimists would call 'cramped as shit'). By the time I had clicked the latch and turned my back to the door Suds was already seated and waiting. I couldn't help but feel like I had walked into some bizarre interview for a job that I never applied for. Everything felt so damn formal. The faint glow from the bulb above allowed the shadows to dance across his face, making his stare all the more sinister as he nodded for me to take a seat. I obeyed.

Suds took his time. Digging his hands into the depths of his pockets he extracted a carton of cigarettes and a crumpled box of matches, scoured through the box to find a match that hadn't snapped in transit, struck along the side of the box and lit the cigarette of his choice, cupping his hand around to encourage the flame. Before dumping the items back in his pocket he extended the pack to me. I declined. I've never been a smoker, and I hardly felt that this was the moment to start. After taking a long drag and exhaling the contents of his lungs into the atmosphere I decided to break the silence.

'Alright, Suds. You got me alone. So you gonna tell

me what's happening? You're spooking me out here.'

'Spooked?' came the low, growling reply. 'Spooked? Spooked ain't enough, Coop. If you knew the half of it you'd need a better word for it than *spooked*.'

I didn't like the tone he took. I sat there confused, hands in my lap like a naughty kid wondering what it was he'd done wrong. What was it that had gotten Suds' back up? Besides from the faint echo of our voices all was silent. Even the murmurs and hums from the bar couldn't make it through the thick walls of this room.

'Then what word would you rather I use? 'Cause I can't really say shit until you tell me what's going on, man. Is it the teasing? I swear, I've been telling them to back off but you know how it is with those guys. One lil joke and that sticks with you for a lifetime. But you don't need to pay it no notice. Ignore it and you'll be fine. Just come out, grab your drinks and finish the night.'

I didn't put much hope into that last bit. I guess I knew deep down that there was just nothing else I could say. I'm not much of a diplomat. That was Pete and Den's job.

Suds looked up to the ceiling, for the first time that night I could see him underneath that harsh exterior. The Suds we knew. A glossy-eyed stare accompanied another exhale of smoke before he rubbed his eyes with the backs of his fists and looked at me. In a way, it comforted me, though his words did less to ease my worry.

'You don't see it yet, Coop. But you will. You're completely oblivious to him, but I can see that there's going to be trouble tonight. I can see it whenever he looks at me, and he knows I know. Shit. There won't be any going back for me, Coop. I just, can't risk being around him no more,' the tears began to well.

'I don't understand.'

'Neither did I. Not until recently. I always knew that there was something in it, in the looks he gave and the way he was, but it never clicked. And it wasn't until I remembered the old times, the stories we used to tell, though I never once dreamed there'd be any truth in them. But as time went on I kept feeling it, deep in my gut, like it was real and I couldn't quite grasp it or place a finger on it. There's always been something haunting me, Coop. Almost following me around, and I could never shake it. Until I saw it in his eyes and I knew then, like I know now. I thought I was losing my mind but I know it's true, and he confirmed it tonight, though he don't know how. All of it. I know all of it now.'

He was rambling, and with each sentence his breath quickened. I found myself struggling to take it all in. *Who?* I kept thinking. What was it and who was it that had brought out this behaviour in Suds?

'Woah, woah. Calm down, Suds. Take a breath. You're not making any sense'.

Instantly he deflated, accepting that more explanation was needed.

'You're right. I'm babbling, I'm sorry. I'll start over. You know you told us how you used to get those dreams about… about your father? Dreams that felt so goddamn real that you said you could almost feel him? Almost like they weren't dreams at all, that they were actual memories of things that happened?'

I nodded.

'Well, recently I've been having the same kind of thing... about... *my* father.'

His words struck me like a lightning bolt, sharpening my attention. Suds was never one to bring up his family, least of all his father. On the few occasions that conversations would park near family he would turn red-faced and tight-lipped at the mere mention of 'daddy'. At one point, Tommy made the mistake of asking if Suds' knew what his father was up to these days and Suds did nothing more than pelt his half-eaten apple at his face, narrowly missing and hitting the wall behind before skulking off. Tommy rose to retaliate but the guys held him back. I guess it was just so out of character for Suds that they all had the good sense to give him his space.

But now he had something to say.

'In all honesty I never really knew who my father was. He disappeared when I was only a kid and Mother seemed so broken up about it all that any time I mentioned him she'd send me to my room and cry. After trying a few times with the same result I never mentioned it again. I mean, if it upset her so, who was I to rehash the past and cause my own mother pain? Folks' mothers and fathers leave all the time right? That's just something you have to get over.'

He looked at me for some kind of response. I just listened.

'Anyway, over the last few months I've been having these dreams. Dreams about the father I never knew. At first they started off hazy, sort of like, I could see him through a fog and I knew it was a dream. Parts of it would skip and I wouldn't get the full tale, which was kinda nice at the time. But as time went on and I started seeing more and more of the dream it became clearer. Felt much more *real*. And the blanks started filling in a piece at a time like an old jigsaw puzzle until a couple of weeks ago I saw the full feature, and now I can't get that shit out my head. Every night I struggle to fall asleep yet he finds me, and every night I have to relive it.'

I find my tongue. 'Tell me about it, Suds. Get it off your chest.'

He paused a moment to refill his lungs with smoke. 'Okay. From the beginning. In the dream I must've been about 4 years old. No more really. I had on a dusty set of dungarees and my father's hat which wobbled around on my tiny head. Father was working in his garage, which seems accurate enough. I remember finding a box full of receipts for car parts with my father's name on them under my mother's bed one day. I guessed he must've been some kinda car fixer-upper though the garage to the side of our house had been cleared years ago and only ever saw use as a rain shelter for me and my friends in the summer storms.

'He was laughing and patting my head, rubbing sausage fingers with grease stains across the suede of the cap, though he didn't seem to mind. He seemed happy. Content. His smile warmed me in that way that only a father's can and I couldn't help but return my own.'

'Sounds like a sweet start to a dream to me', I said.

'Like you say, Coop. It's the start.' He continued, 'I remember feeling the heat of the sun bearing down on us, frying us in the yard like eggs in a pan. It must've been high-heat of the summer as it hurt to catch the sun even out the corner of your eye. So father picked me up, threw me over his shoulders and dragged me into the shade of the workshop, placing me gently on an empty crate. He bent his knees, wiped my brow and called for mother to bring us both some drinks from the house – we were thirsty boys that needed our engines topped up after all. Mother strode across the yard, hair tied back in that long ponytail she was famous for and handed us our glasses. Even in my sleep I can taste the sweet nectar of that homemade lemonade. Ain't nothing like your mother's own recipes, eh?

"'Hope you boys are playing nice," she'd tease. "Hot, sunny day like this could shorten anyone's fuse in a hurry."

"'Can't nothing stop a man smiling on a day like today, hon. Especially with my little worker helping me out. I've got more done this morning than I managed all last week. Who knew all I needed was an apprentice?" Then he'd shoot a wink my way.

"'I expect nothing less from my little angel. Who knows, if you work real hard and let daddy teach you a thing or two you could be as big and strong as him one day." She'd blow us both a kiss and walk back into the house with a skip in her step.

'Then this is the part where it starts to change.

'At this point, I don't know why, the sky would begin shifting. Grey and black clouds would start popping up on the bright blue of the sky, dotting the painted landscape like acne on a teenage girl. Father would look up to the sky and make some comment about how *God must be a woman with all these mood swings*, then laugh to himself, face-deep in the rusty engine of some old, black vehicle. I'd still be sat on my box, swinging my legs and waiting in anticipation for the rain to come. There was always something in the way that the water would thud lightly on the dirt, marking its territory with a dark splodge that relaxed me. I'd stand, walk out from the shelter of the garage roof and hold out my arms, grinning from ear to ear, waiting for the rain to come – and it did.

'When it started, it would always come straight to me. *Plip, plop, plip, plop*. Arms outstretched, I'd attempt to catch every drop that fell. As a toddler, it's easy to get lost in the simplicity of it, that's the beauty at that age, everything is new, everything is fresh, everything is *holy*. And I would stand and spin, like a Jesus Christ spinning top, twirling as the rain began to increase its force. I'd soak in the damp, warm smell that rose from the ground beneath my dancing feet and listen to the *pitter, patter* as my clothes grew heavier with each rotation.

'And then he'd come.'

With shaking hands he took a few long, deep drags to calm himself, with little effect. You could see Suds growing apprehensive at whatever it was to come next. I circled the table, seating myself next to the guy looking like he was fighting back tears. My arm draped over his shoulder as I asked, 'Who came?' For all the thinking in my head, I couldn't imagine what could break such a sweet dream.

Composing himself he wiped his nose, closed his eyes and continued.

'I would lose myself in the flurry of my spinning, only stopping at the point where I was so dizzy that I'd fall down. Behind me I could hear my father hammering on some part or other, releasing a rhythmic metallic clank into the atmosphere. Above, the sky would be all swirls of black and grey as the clouds began rolling and tumbling, loosing raindrops that, at this point, had grown close to the size of grapes. I'd look up and see pulses of what I can only imagine to be electricity. Tiny, barely visible to begin with. Swimming through the clouds as tiny insects the pulses would grow as, with each *clang*, *clang*, *clang*, they would collide at a central point in the sky which grew steadily brighter as the seconds passed. My heart would be racing as I watched the lights dance in the atmosphere. I guess through the whole performance a part of me – that part that lives in the real world – would scream at my sleeping self to seek shelter, to go into the house where mother would be safe and dry, basking in the warmth that spilled out the oven as she prepared dinner for her two boys. But that's not how dreams work.

'I know it all now. Each step is predictable, only to me, yet inescapable. A nightmare that I have to live through knowing every part as it's about to happen. Watching it again and again and wishing I could run. Wishing that I could snap my fingers and wake up the minute the electric pulses culminated in their crescendo, the second that the lightning exploded from the centre of the sky, the moment the sound of the light crashing through the garage roof would deafen my infantile ears and I'd scream a scream that I couldn't even hear as my father collapsed to the floor in a haze of smoke and a smell of burned flesh.

'I'd run, though in the nightmare it would feel like walking. I'd wish for my muscles to find the energy to run to Father but none would come. Though I'd be making progress, waving my arms in front to clear the smoke that shrouded us, I could never get their fast enough. It was like the barricade of black fog would be working against me, taunting me, grabbing the backs of my legs with long, ethereal tendrils that seemed determined to trip me and stop me from reaching my goal. Somehow, despite the aching in my limbs, I'd find him. Every time I'd wish that I hadn't.'

I squeezed his shoulder as his words trailed off. I was at a loss to find something to say that would comfort the poor soul – to have to watch your father get struck and burned nightly is no way to live. Though I could say that I'd be happy to see my old man suffer for leaving, it certainly wasn't the way for everyone. And as we sat in that hauntingly quiet room with nothing but the echo of Suds' sniffs and the vague buzzing from the overhead lamp I couldn't help but wonder, as horrible as the visions may have been, why was he telling me this?

'That's horrible. That's no way for any man to go. Least of all your Pa. Just remember, Suds… it was all just a dream.'

*

I couldn't remember the point at which I'd started crying. Not heavy tears, mind, just enough to feel the puffiness above my cheeks and to notice the booth through a hazy blur. I suppose in many ways it's impossible to ride on the back of last night and come out the tunnel unscathed, but I have to admit that this is the first time I've lost control and allowed the salty liquid to run since Pa left. Something about Suds' story struck a nerve in me, even at that point where I still had hope that the night could go on.

I feel the shame grow inside me as I remember that I'm not alone. That buddy next door will be able to see me as I rub my eyes on the cleanest part of my sleeve I can find, leaving darkened smears over the brown splatters of dried blood. That stale, earthy smell finding its way back into my nostrils.

I look once more at him – God's servant – bound to spend his remaining days, hours, confined to four walls that would struggle to hold an embrace. Listening to the sinners and pricks of the world and abdicating each and every one of their weights that burden their shoulders. How do you decide that your time is worth the clocks of the bastards that can't find the time in the day to help others in return?

*

'You don't understand, Coop.' He threw my arm off and stood, pacing the limits of the space like a caged circus lion hungry for freedom. 'That's not how he died.' The look was back in his eye, that combination of fear and anger that could turn any neighbourhood citizen into an unpredictable monster. His voice had grown louder, begging to be heard, understood, and I was trying my best. Dear God, I was trying.

'But... you said—'

'The lightning didn't kill him, Coop. Although I wish it had. He should've died then and there. The sound of the crashing, the intensity of that strike would be enough to take down a goddamn ox on steroids, but it didn't. In my hurry to find his body through the smoke I tripped over my uncoordinated feet and smacked my head on the floor – hard. My hands reached blindly out to find his presumed corpse and my fingers found nothing. No body, no clothing, no nothing. I couldn't understand. It was too much to process and my head throbbed from the force of what was sure to be some kind of concussion. Tears exploded from my face as I screamed and screamed for father, for mother, for someone to help me. Eventually he came. A sharp tug on the back of my collar lifted me clean off the ground, and as he spun me to face him I froze.

'For it was my father, in most respects. He was wearing the same blue jumpsuit smothered in grease stains and frays (and an additional few scorch marks), he had his heavy-set ankle boots with the hardened toe-caps, and thick gloves. Though it wasn't him, all the same. He was... *smoking*. Not from any kinda cig between his teeth, but from his toes to his head a light grey vapour leaked into the atmosphere as though he was burning from the inside. And as I looked into his eyes it was confirmed, for staring straight at me I could see the familiar features of his face, emitting unfamiliar depths of fire. Where his crystal blues used to stand a blackness swallowed the space, filling even the whites of his eyes. Within the abyss a fire gently flickered. On another occasion I might've said this was comforting, reminding me of the old log fire we'd sit around in winter, were it not accompanied by the emptiness of his gaze, and that grin that I only ever used to get a peek at late at night when Father used it on Mother after he'd been drinking and she wasn't in the mood. Protruding from his lips his tongue danced, allowing a denser cloud of smoke to fog his face. He was tasting the air. I wasn't sure what for.

'I'd lash and shake and wriggle, attempting to free myself from the iron grip on my neck, noticing then how cold his fingers were to the touch, before resigning myself to his capture. He'd wait until the moment I'd given up before he spoke, in a tone unlike his own, spewing forth from barbecued lips.

'"Hold still, son. Let Daddy get a good look at you." He pulled me closer to his face and I could feel the pressure intensify from the heat as the smell of charred flesh invaded my nostrils. His nails dug into the back of my neck, piercing the skin and I felt the warm blood trail down my spine. "You've been a naughty boy, haven't you?"

'I'd shake my head. I'd always been a good kid, a mummy's boy for the most part.

'"Lies!" He'd scream at me before throwing me to

the floor, advancing with slow, deliberate steps. I'd kick my legs to push backwards as quickly as I could, slipping occasionally on the grease-stained floor, stopping only once the cold metal of the workshop walls met my back and blocked my escape.

'My younger self would scream at the fiery figure as he approached with that hungry look in his eye. I'd feel my throat restrict as my voice grew harsher as the smoke found its way inside me, denying my lungs of oxygen. I'd wonder where Mother was as my vision would start to blur and I'd become light-headed, watching the ashy silhouette of my father expand and grow until all I knew was darkness.

'I never know how long I go out for, or what truly happened after that. But I would awake to the gentle voice of my mother shaking my shoulder as she tried to fight back tears. Behind her the Sheriff would stand next to the figure of my father, hunched over his knees, no longer accompanied by the thick trail of smoke and looking as dazed and confused as can be.

'And that was the last I'd see of him. There's never an opportunity for me to say goodbye, and it wasn't until recently that I discovered the town sent him out for a lynching. I know it was for the best. But it's never easy learning the truth of your family history, and I get why Mother used to cry so much now.'

I looked to Suds, confused at his change in tone. 'Hold on, you're confusing it Suds. It was all a dream remember? What's all this chatter about "recently discovering"? I know dreams can sometimes *feel* real, but this kinda story would fit well in one of them fantasy books Pete keeps reading.'

It was then that Suds shifted forward in his seat and pulled the collar at his back low enough to reveal the marks. Four small, adjacent reminders glinting silvery in the lamplight. Scars to serve as memories.

I suppose at that point I just stared. As my mind worked overtime to process it all I thought back to all the tales and stories I'd heard as a kid. Sure, there was always the possibility that the overactive imagination of youth would paint a story different or change it slightly. It was then that I realised that I'd heard this story before.

'Suds...' I began, careful to choose my words right. 'That story they used to tell at school... that one about Mr Thrisket and his demon boy... sounds an awful lot like your dream, but kinda... reversed?' I'm not sure what I expected, but it sure as hell wasn't a smile.

'Nice to meet you, Cooper. I'm Karl,' he said, extending an arm out to me.

I slapped his hand away. 'C'mon Suds, I know your name.'

'Karl *Thrisket*.' His smile faded, along with mine.

We sat for a moment in silence, Suds allowing his words to work in my head. '*Thrisket*...' I began. 'So, you're—'

'Davy Thrisket's son, in the flesh.'

'Which means—'

'Weren't no dream, Cooper. It's a memory.'

Confused, I repeated, 'But the story I heard was the other way round. They said it was the *boy* had the devil in him, and his papa was trying to beat it out.'

'Course they'd say that, Coop. S'more comforting

to anyone looking to believe a story that the guy was *crazy* rather than possessed. Grown man fries his brain, sees the devil in his kid, goes nuts, hung, story over. Sounds a lot better than some kind of demon jumping his body, huh? That kinda shit would unsettle the town and need quite a bit of explaining, wouldn't you agree?'

I nodded. Even though it made sense it didn't make it any easier to digest. As a kid I'd spent years believing in ghost tales and horror stories. I'd take any chance I could to hear the horrors that people spewed my way, and I revelled in the telling. Tales of slime monsters rising from the swamp, vampires waiting at the door, werewolves, ghouls. You name it, I'd heard it – and I believed it all. Even went on a couple of ghost runs myself, trekking to places that were told to be haunted and spending the night camping, praying for a glimpse of something to appear. But nothing would ever come, and eventually I lost my faith in the supernatural.

Then there was this. This... tale... pouring from the heart of a familiar face. I guess that's how I saw it then. I couldn't argue with him really, and I didn't want to. Something in the way he told it made it real, made me believe. And, in all honesty, I wanted to leave it then and there, console the poor bastard and help him on his way home. But there was something that I couldn't really shuffle, that kinda feeling that comes to you late at night, when the lights are off and you hear a scuffling in the corner of your room, knowing that it ain't shit but your mind playing tricks, but you turn your light on anyway.

'Why tonight? You say you've been having this... dream... for a few months now. What is it that's got you so spooked tonight of all nights?'

'Coop... It's Den—'

A loud knock on the door was swiftly followed by the wobbling head of Pete. I had no idea how long we'd been in that room, but the effects of the alcohol were apparent behind his half-seeing eyes. He didn't seem to pay attention to the puffiness of Suds' eyes and the sticky trails where the tears had run.

'There you are!' he slurred, spraying booze-laced spit into the room, looking more surprised at the fact that he was standing than at the presence of his targets before him. 'Rushty said we could shtay pasht closhe, but we're lea-*hick*-ving now. Dennish is out for the count, and you know the rulesh, Coop.' I want to say that he winked at me, but it came out as a crooked blink.

We always had an unbroken bond. A set of rules to make sure that we always had each other's backs, and could always count on another to keep us safe. We'd pair up. Nice and simple. If ever we found ourselves in a situation where one of us would need looking after we had picked a designated person to be responsible for us. Bound in blood, me and Dennis were the first to pair.

'Sure thing, Pete. Go sleep it off.' He waved his arm in a drunken salute and slammed the door behind him.

I looked then to Suds, noticing how tired he appeared. Shadows jigged across his face highlighting the bags that hung from his eyes like rain-soaked hammocks. Silently I communicated. *Wait there, I'll just check on Dennis.* Silently, he answered. *Don't.* I paid him no heed.

Turning the handle I pulled the door open and stepped into the stillness of the empty bar. The fellas had switched off the lights allowing the silver moon to cast its silky glow over the polished surfaces that scattered the room. I followed the path to our table and sat next to my companion only then noticing that the table was empty and that I sat alone. I looked about the bar finding no discernible silhouette of a sleeping patron, but a quick look at the floor found the presence of a dense mist as it began to thicken and crawl upwards.

Quicker than a kid caught tugging himself I shot to my feet, searching wildly for Dennis. My mind immediately jumping back to Suds' story and the horror that he faced. *Dennis! Where are you?* I struggled to say out loud, the words reverberating inside my skull. *Suds?!* As my eyes once again found the door marked PRIVATE I caught movement out of the corner of my eye. Through the darkness I found him, his silver-lined silhouette sat on the counter of the bar. A sharp pain shot through my hand causing me to briefly double over. His stare was intense, burning into my core. I knew something was wrong, out of place. Even at his worst Dennis could always manage a smile. Its absence from his face as he sat, hunched over, swaying his legs over the bar locked my knees and rooted me where I stood.

'There you are!' I shouted, trying to act casual. Hoping that some levity would hide the shaking in my voice. 'Was worried about you, Den. Pete said the drink had knocked you out for the night, seems he must've been drunker than you are.' Eyes staring. 'Still, I ain't never seen a fish drink so much as you tonight. Why don't we head home and you can sleep it off?'

When he spoke it was without a slur, a congressman at the podium.

'Well, Pete was never one to hold his liquor now, was he? Seems he should learn to look after himself before worrying about others. He should know I've always been able to handle myself.' His sobriety was unnerving. 'I saw you and Suds having a little chat in the back. I hope he wasn't putting stories in your head.' A flicker of red flashed across his eyes as the corner of his mouth curled into a demented smile. We both knew he knew, and we both knew that our encounter was monitored by an hourglass very quickly running out of sand. For a split second my mind jumped back to Suds, wondering what he was doing, remembering the look in his eyes as I left and closed the door behind me. Was he hiding?

Dennis seemed to read my thoughts. 'I wouldn't hold out hope for old Suds there, Coop. He may have escaped daddy, but you know as well as I do his sacks are emptier than a barrel in a drought. It's just you and me against the world, just how we always dreamed it. Ain't that right?' He stood then, losing his feet in the growing abyss. As the fire behind his lids began to glow with excitement my legs found the strength to stumble backwards.

'That's how it always was, Dennis. Me and you, you and me. I always had your back, and you always had mine.' Dennis beamed at me, smoke seeping from between his teeth as that familiar tingle returned to my palm.

In a flash the figure of Dennis collapsed into the mist, swallowed by the silky waves, before reforming only inches from my face. The heat from his breath hit me like a bag of sand as he stood, showcasing that award-winning smile that made so many ladies weak at the knees. My knees trembled for different reasons. I knew where this was headed. I'd just heard the story. Though the key details of how Suds managed to escape were missing, and I felt helpless to figure my own way. A warmth began to creep down my thigh as the force of his laugh shot away the dewy beads and dried the tears forming on my face.

'And that's how it can all remain, dear friend – dear *brother* – should you choose the path of the wise.' His voice was smoky, seductive. He reached forward and caressed my face with an ice-cold hand in a way familiar to lovers. Though underneath it all I could feel the control of something beyond Dennis. Something unholy. *Unnatural*. A puppeteer without strings.

'What path would that be?' I spoke in a voice without substance.

'Join me, Coop,' he whispered, lips against my ear as I quivered on the spot. Words picked for me. 'Help me finish what was started and join me on the path of the eternal. Everything that you have ever desired lays in this choice, with me. Shake off your misgivings and join me, Coop. We can be brothers, unstoppable, forever.'

Unwillingly my thoughts turned to my father, gone. Wondering where his fate rested. Wondering whether he was alive or dead on his journey without responsibility. What if I could see him again? I could ask the questions

I never had the chance to, I could find the answers that have plagued my childhood and aged my crippled mother beyond her years. For grief has the power to forward the clocks. Could all of this really be possible with the power that was holding my friend? Sure, stories tell of fire and shadows as negative, but what if we're wrong? What if there really was a hope beyond this that would create happiness beyond measure? The excitement was building within me and I could feel the presence leaving Dennis, I could see his pearly whites gleaming towards me, the lines and shadows on his face all but gone as I saw the Dennis that I met at school standing before me. The Coyote was melting, flooded with light as dreamscapes of sunny days in the playground returned. We were two innocent youths, surrounded by the buzz and whirlwind of children playing. A ball flew by my head as a familiar face with a name lost to the past sped by leaving a trail of laughter to the wind. And there, standing behind Dennis's beaming face he stood. Wavy hair haphazardly tucked behind his ear, his favourite blue collared shirt, chewing his favourite tobacco – my father as I remember him to be. My voice escaped to the wind as I looked towards his smiling face and he crouched low, holding his arms out wide in the way he used to. My feet began to move slowly, cautiously as my mind fought battles tougher than an elephant's hide.

He came out of nowhere, crashing and splintering, raining droplets of wood over my vision, dissolving the light and painting back the darkness. All feeling of hope instantly shattered as Suds stood panting, eyes wide, holding the remnants of the chair that hadn't shattered against Dennis's skull.

'Suds!— '

'Save it, Coop. Let's get the fuck out of here!' urgency stained his words as his eyes darted around the room. It was then that I noticed that Dennis had disappeared. For how long? We had no idea.

Any shred of energy that remained was spent in that moment, bankrupting my reserves as adrenaline fuelled my legs and we darted for the door, throwing aside any obstacle that blocked our way until we were only a metre away. But he beat us. Of course he did. And he boldly stood as the final obstruction before our freedom.

'My, my. What's the hurry?' he teased, dragging his words with a smile. 'It's such a shame that you couldn't see sense, Coop. I had such hope for you. I'm sure your mother will be very disappointed in you.' I didn't like the emphasis he held on those last words.

I took a sideways glance at Suds and found his eyes set. His mind made up. He knew it was fruitless for himself to try to escape. Looking into my eyes I saw the same look my father gave me all those years ago as he tucked me into bed, said goodnight and left the bedroom never to return. He was sacrificing himself.

Before I had the chance to say anything he swung – hard – catching the chair leg against the door as Dennis dodged and returned to the mist. My hand shot for the door handle, noticing then how the mist, thick as treacle, resisted its opening. Somehow I managed to squeeze through the gap into the cold night air and relished the oxygen that filled my lungs. Without a second thought I began to sprint like never before, kicking up a dusty cloud into the dark night.

*

From a distance I can hear the low whirring of sirens. Flashy red and blues that signal the arrival of so-called justice. In my head I can see them now. The heavy moustache of the leading officer and his eager, young sidekick, chasing the deliberate trail I left behind. Steppin' Wolf's *Born to be Wild* echoing across the landscape as they chase the unknown. It was only a matter of time before they'd catch up. It was all too messy, and I'd never been one to clean up my after myself. I guess I got that from Pa. That man was the worst kind of slob. Though I guess his leaving should have made it all the easier for Ma to keep the place tidy, somehow it had the opposite effect. Her grief hit her hard and she never really lost his ghost, soon becoming too sick to tidy after herself. It all goes full circle I suppose. A cataclysmic circle of life.

The sweat is pouring off my forehead like holy water at a christening, and I once again wonder how much of my story Preacher has taken in. His breathing, deep and heavy, gently rocks his body as his impossible patience gives me the strength to carry on. I assure him that I'm nearly done.

The sirens are getting closer.

*

A scream pierced the blackness of the night causing even the moon to hide behind the comfort of the clouds. It seemed impossible that such a sound could come from the throat of a grown man, but as I turned around, noticing that in my rush Suds hadn't kept pace, my heart dropped. From the doorway of the Coyote he stood, cloaked in Dennis's foggy embrace.

Producing the deep, heavy bassline of the fatal soundtrack Dennis's laughter boomed as the red flames of his eyes shone like guiding beacons in the dark. My bladder unloaded the remainder of its contents as I just watched, willing my brain to come up with some way to help, something to save Suds from the smoky grave.

'Dennis! Take me,' the words sprang involuntarily. I could see the stars reflected in Suds' water-filled eyes, shimmering like tiny fireflies. 'Take me. We're *brothers* Dennis. Take me.'

'Oh, Coop,' he drawled, topping up his grin. 'But I already have you.' The pain returned to my hand forcing my eyes to look away as the final cry of death shot into the air and awakened the night. By the time my eyes found the doorway to the Coyote Suds lay lost in the mist. Dennis was nowhere to be seen.

I wish I could say that I ran to his body, that I sprinted like hell to check for a pulse, but I didn't. Before I could even think of taking those steps towards him I saw the blood trailing down the steps and I knew it was too late. Suds was lost. Taken to a place beyond explanation. I turned on my heels taking the first steps towards putting as much distance between me and whatever-the-fuck-Dennis-was and ran for home. Ran for comfort. Ran for Ma.

My feet hit the ground harder than a thunder clap as I remembered the emphasis Dennis placed on her name. Somehow I knew that I'd be racing the clock and was suffering a hefty disadvantage. Not knowing whether I'd make it home in time to see the life in my Ma's eyes one more time before death came and took her hand in hand with Suds. The standalone townhouses rushed by, each nothing but a blurry shadow as my feet moved faster than they had ever known.

I nearly fell flat as I hurled myself up the porch steps to the front door. The house stood in complete darkness as I jumped into the living room and shouted for Ma. My words were met with silence, though I have to admit that I was thankful that I could see the floor, clear as day. I prayed a silent blessing for each wooden tile that met my vision, unobscured by that ominous fog. My breathing calmed whilst my brain (as it so often does when met with a situation beyond comprehension) began to doubt my recent encounter, blaming alcohol for pushing my imagination into overdrive.

Something gentle stroked my ear, barely noticeable, followed by a shimmer of light that bounced off the doorway to the kitchen. Taking extra care to camouflage myself with the quiet of the house I cautiously made my way to the threshold. Small notches lined the wooden doorframe – childhood reminders of our heights growing up. I peered inside.

Besides the twinkles and reflections of the night everything seemed to be in place. The standard pile of dishes that sought refuge on the sideboard climbed precariously high, the sink held greasy water that dazzled in bruise colours in the night, and the gentle dripping of the tap softly played its *drip, drip, drip*, magnified by the silence of the house. Leaning against the frame of the door I rubbed my eyes. My hands slipped against the sweat that lined my forehead and for an instant the world was dark, absorbed behind the rough skin of my fingers as they attempted to massage the dull ache that remained thumping in my head.

After a few moments my thoughts gathered enough to remind myself that even though the house was empty, the house was *empty*. I had seen no sign yet to fully reassure me that Ma was okay. As I turned from the kitchen to check the rest of the house I noticed that the dripping noise was becoming louder the closer I moved to the stairs. A quick look back confirmed the absence of water leaving the tap as the fear returned.

I moved towards the bottom of the stairs. Time stood still in that moment. Black mist descended over my eyes and fogged my dizzy head as flashes and images flickered across my sight like an old movie projector. I knew what lay ahead. I know it sounds cliché, but my life flashed before my eyes. Images of Ma and Pa sat on the porch, watching the sun set as me and Kenny raced each other around the garden; all of us sat around the kitchen table laughing and discussing the trivial shit that families do; the day Pa left; the slow deterioration of Ma's spine as the house crumbled along with her marriage.

The blood was unmissable. Dark, liquid trails snaking their way down each step like a satanic waterfall. I dared not look to the top. Not all at once, for I feared that it may be too much for me to take – but I made my way to her. Each step felt like a lifetime. Not giving a shit about my ever-slickening shoes against the hard surface of the stairs my prayers escaped my lips, begging for my prediction to not be realised. Though I saw. First sight was her delicate feet, encased in her light night-shoes, thick and laden with the slowly congealing blood that coated the material. Next, her shins, exposed from her awkward seating position at the top of the stairs where she spent countless nights waiting for Pa to return. After, her nightdress, cream-turned-red, clinging to the skeletal shape of her legs as they impossibly supported her structure. Her hips, her shoulders, hunched over like that buzzard waiting for its kill – ironic. Finally, her eyes, darkened from the absence of life, yet somehow watchful, somehow laced with a relief that can only come from the removal of worldly pains. As rigor mortis held her infinite position like a queen immortalised atop a mountain, I couldn't help sharing her relief. Knowing that, wherever she was, it had to be better for her. She was free.

Unable to turn my glance away from the blackened coals that dotted where Ma's eyes had once been, I noticed two things in quick succession. First, the throbbing that had ailed my head now directed its attention to my palm. Second, the cold iron of the coals began to glow anew with tiny embers, as though someone from deep inside Ma was stoking the fire.

A cackle. A twitch. A shove as he shot forth from Ma's lifeless form and tossed me down the stairs.

In an instant Dennis had me pinned, straddling me like a cheap whore and roared waves of heat and ash towards my face. My eyelids blocked the worst of it, though when I managed to look once more at his smug features I felt all hope abandon the ship of my body.

'I gave you a choice, Cooper. You should've helped me. You should've been on my side,' he spoke, hurt at my abandonment. I struggled against his iron grip. 'There's no use struggling. Wherever you go, I go. We're bound together, *remember*? That's how it's always been. Ever since we were kids.' He extended a smoke-laden arm towards my face, holding out his palm. All heat, smoke and ash cleared a small perimeter circling his hand, an island in a volcano, and I saw then the small, silver tattoo that matched my own.

'See, Coop? We're blood broth—'

Knowing where the tool was made it all the easier as, wrenching my arm free, I whipped my hand round to the extra pocket that hung from Pa's chair, released his switchblade and pierced the exposed flesh under Dennis's chin. At that point anger, fear and grief took over as the blade danced in and out of Dennis like the needle of a sewing machine allowing smoke and blood to combine as it poured out of each wound. His scream fell unmatched against my own as I let the knife sing a song of its own language over the corpse of my former best friend. Even now I can see the surprise on his face as he metamorphosed before my eyes. The fire that burned inside his body shook loose and slithered through the floorboards leaving Dennis to return to his true form, now heavy against the gravitational pull of death as he flopped onto my body. Not knowing what else to do I held his body in an apologetic embrace.

The house fell into silence once more.

*

I can hear car doors slamming outside. The sirens have ground to a halt yet the lights continue to scan through the stains of the window adding to the cornucopia of colour that dazzles the booth. With the sun confident in its sky residency I can see the world outside the glass of the chapel in full technicolour. The officers have taken off their hats allowing their balding heads to cool in the heat as they stroll around my muck-covered car, writing notes on tiny pads of paper. I now know that I have no hope of leaving this looking like the good guy. Replaying the story back has allowed me to see how it all looks, to see what it might sound like from the other side, and positive is not the word I'd use to describe it. Is it all my fault? No. Not in the slightest. Yet I don't believe the officers may have the patience to hear this story. And what evidence have I got in my corner? Nothing. Just Dennis's blood stains on my shirt and the fact that I fled the scene.

Fuck you, Kenny. Fuck you.

Sure, we've never exactly been sidekicks in a superhero movie, but I thought our bond stretched far enough that he'd give me the benefit of the doubt. That he'd give me the chance to get a word in edgeways when he opened the door, Sarah in tow, giggling like a couple of horny teens hungry for a spanking and saw me struggling to lift Dennis's bloody corpse from me. Pa's knife fell out my hand when he opened the door and his jaw dropped so low I was worried he'd lick the blood off the floor. With a quick command he sent Sarah upstairs (little knowing what crowned the top) and after the screams and some heated shouting he pulled out his gun and I ran for the car. I drove for the hills and found this place.

I guess that old saying fits well here. *You made your bed, you lie in it*. Though, in truth, I feel more like a guest at a messed up hotel. It was never my bed, but here I lie.

In the parking lot outside I see the two officers confirming what they thought. Yes, it's my car. Yes, I'm inside. They check their guns, signal to each other, crouch and advance.

I turn for the last time to see the old preacher's face. Worn, sweating, patient. I look at the silver scar that lines my palm, a reminder of the blood oath we shared. Steam rises from the mark transforming slowly into blackness as the scar burns with a fire I can bear. Closing my eyes I feel myself slip gently down into the familiar thick, dark mist that enshrouds and pulls me under. When I open them once more I have risen and Father Harrison stands before me.

I see the tears in his eyes as he looks at me. Not fear, but *recognition*. The name *Harrison* fades instantly from the preacher figure as my heart begins to race. His features now crystal-clear before my eyes I remember every angle of his face. Every mole and mark. A million thoughts cross my mind as I remember the pain that he once caused us, and I think to everything that I had ever wanted to say whenever he appeared in my dreams. Though the words fail to come.

Despite my anger and confusion, one word leaves my lips as a tear rolls down my cheek.

'Pa?

DANIEL WILLCOCKS

JOIN THE
VIP READERS CLUB

3 FREE STORIES
DISCOUNTS
UPDATES ON NEW RELEASES
BEHIND-THE-SCENES

WWW.DANIELWILLCOCKS.COM

ALSO FROM HAWK & CLEAVER

www.hawkandcleaver.com

Made in the USA
Columbia, SC
05 March 2021